A Gift For: _____

From: _____

*For daddy bears everywhere*
A R

*For Jeff, for your love and encouragement*
A E

# Me and My Dad!

Alison Ritchie

illustrated by Alison Edgson

LITTLE TIGER PRESS

Hallmark
GIFT BOOKS

My dad wakes me up
every morning, like this —
He tickles my nose and
gives me a kiss.

We go out exploring,
there's so much to see.
My dad knows where all
the best secrets will be!

My dad is a giant –
up here so am I –
If I stretch really high
'til I touch the sky.

We find sticky honey,
our favorite snack.
Watch my dad run when the
bees want it back!

My dad twirls me 'round
and the world whizzes past.
My head gets all dizzy,
I'm spinning so fast!

If loud thunder roars
and the skies turn to gray,
My dad keeps me safe
'til the storm goes away.

When it's raining my dad
plays a staying-dry trick –
To dodge all the raindrops
we have to be quick!

We race to the river
and Dad jumps straight in.
I climb on his back
and we go for a swim.

My dad is so strong,
he can lift anything.
I hope I'm strong, too, when
I'm grown-up like him.

When I get sleepy,
Dad gives me a hug
And carries me home,
all cozy and snug.

My dad tells me stories
as day turns to night.
We cuddle up close
in the warm twinkling light.

My dad is the best
daddy bear there could be.
We're together forever —
my dad and me.